Meet Clara

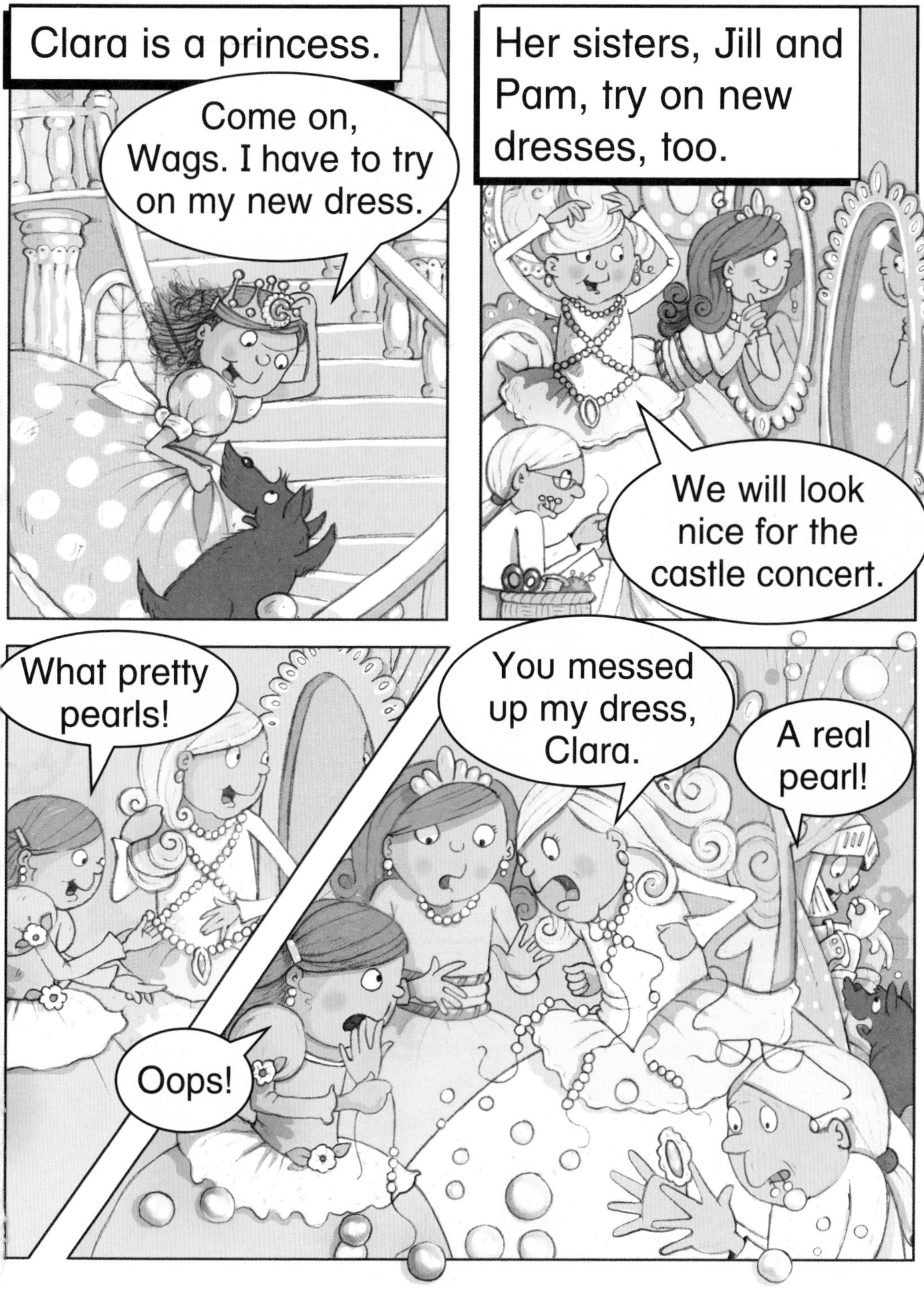
Clara is a princess.
Come on, Wags. I have to try on my new dress.
Her sisters, Jill and Pam, try on new dresses, too.
We will look nice for the castle concert.
What pretty pearls!
You messed up my dress, Clara.
A real pearl!
Oops!

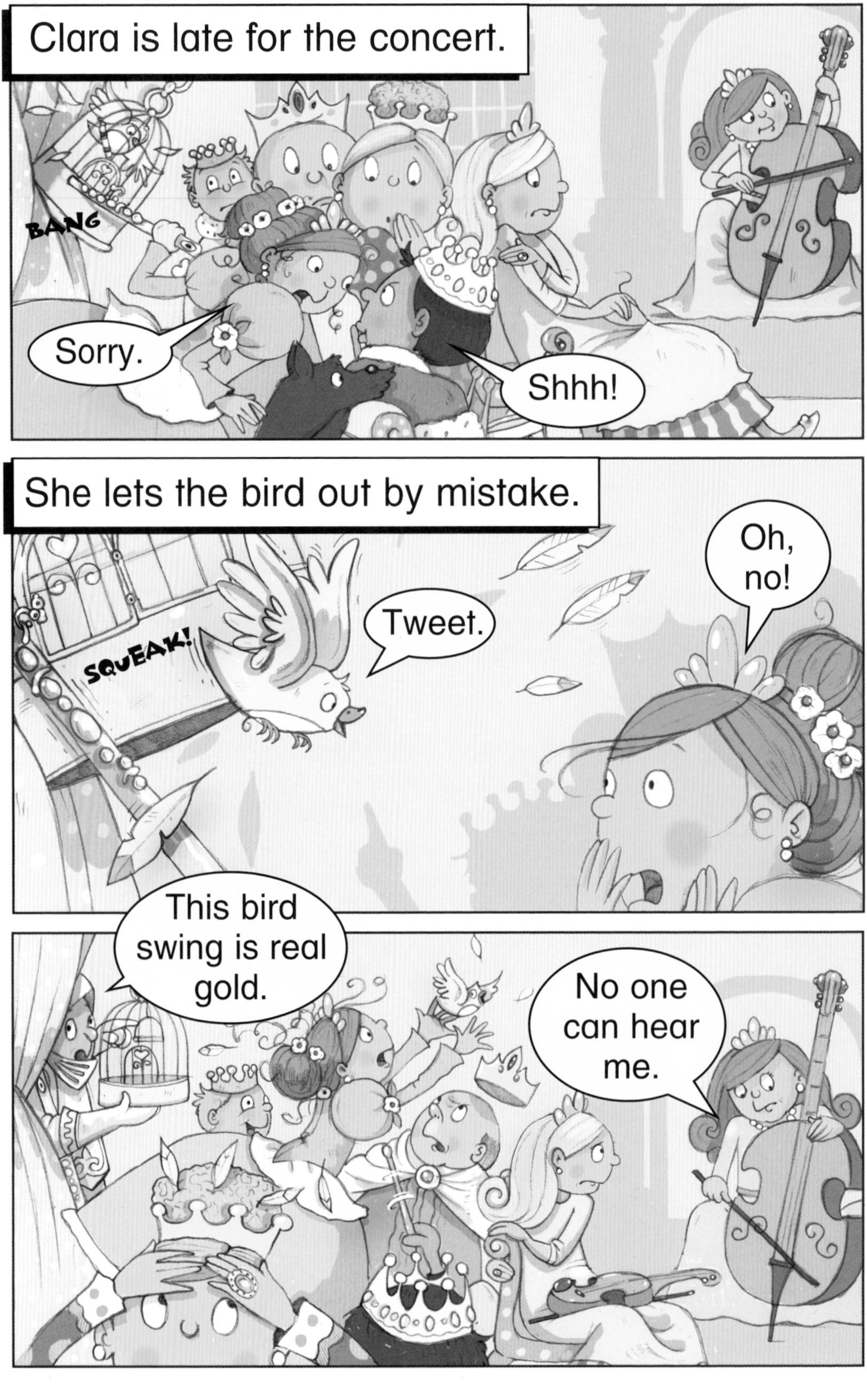
Clara is late for the concert.
BANG
Sorry.
Shhh!
She lets the bird out by mistake.
SQUEAK!
Tweet.
Oh, no!
This bird swing is real gold.
No one can hear me.

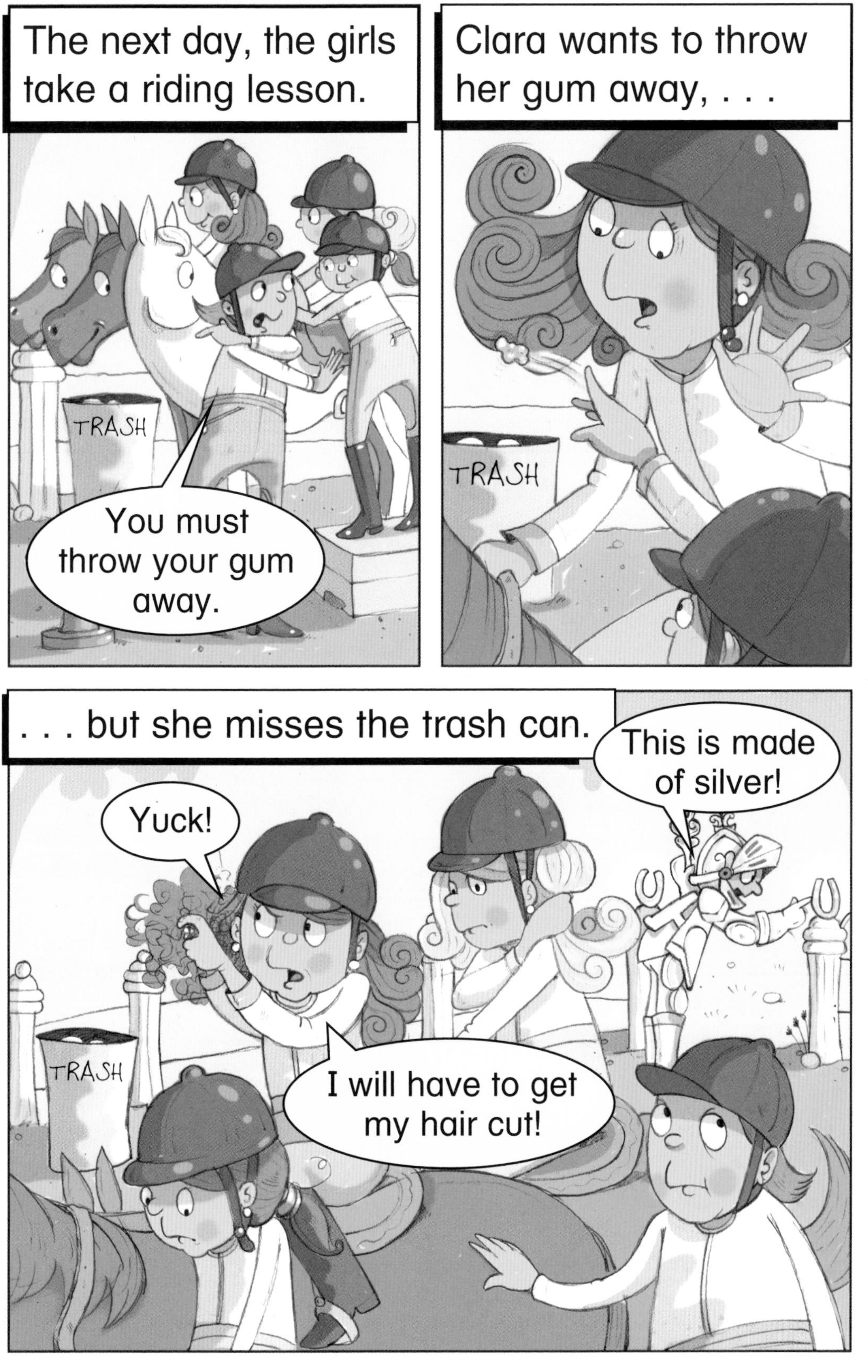
The next day, the girls take a riding lesson.
TRASH
You must throw your gum away.
Clara wants to throw her gum away, . . .
TRASH
. . . but she misses the trash can.
Yuck!
This is made of silver!
TRASH
I will have to get my hair cut!

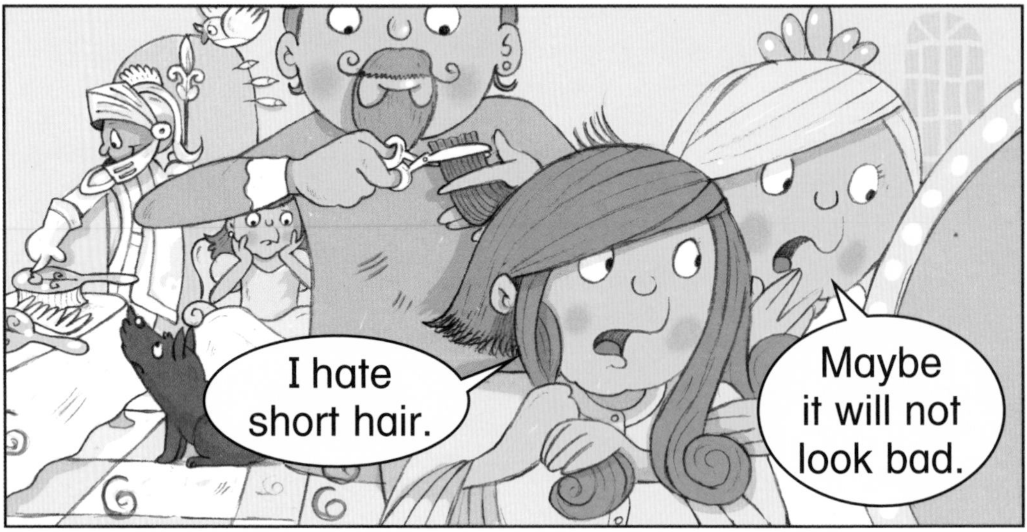
I hate
short hair.
Maybe
it will not
look bad.

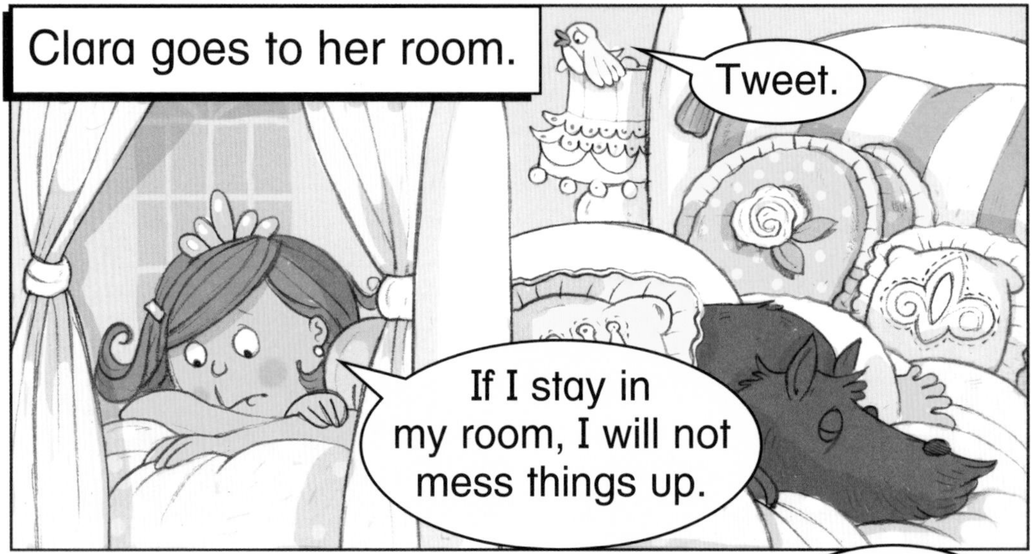
Clara goes to her room.
Tweet.
If I stay in
my room, I will not
mess things up.

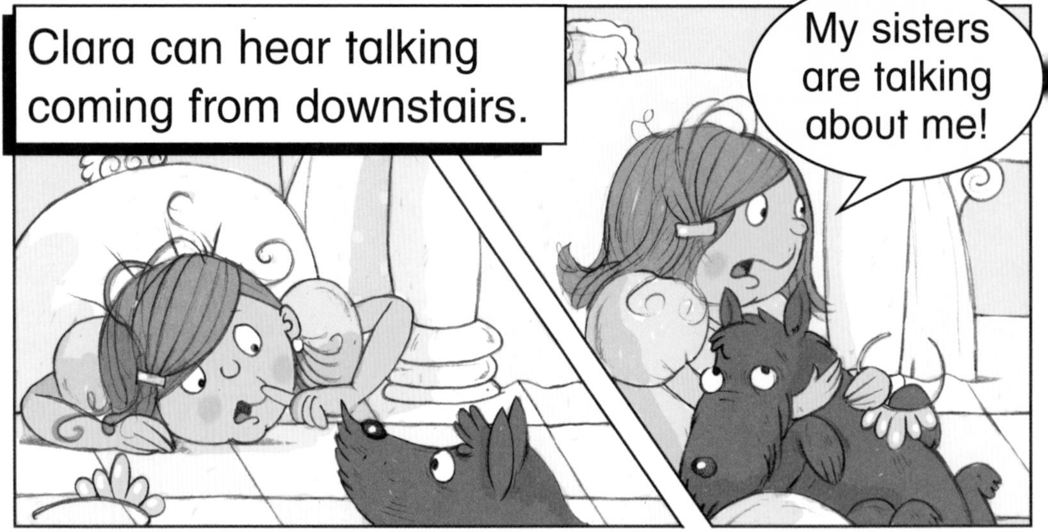
Clara can hear talking
coming from downstairs.
My sisters
are talking
about me!

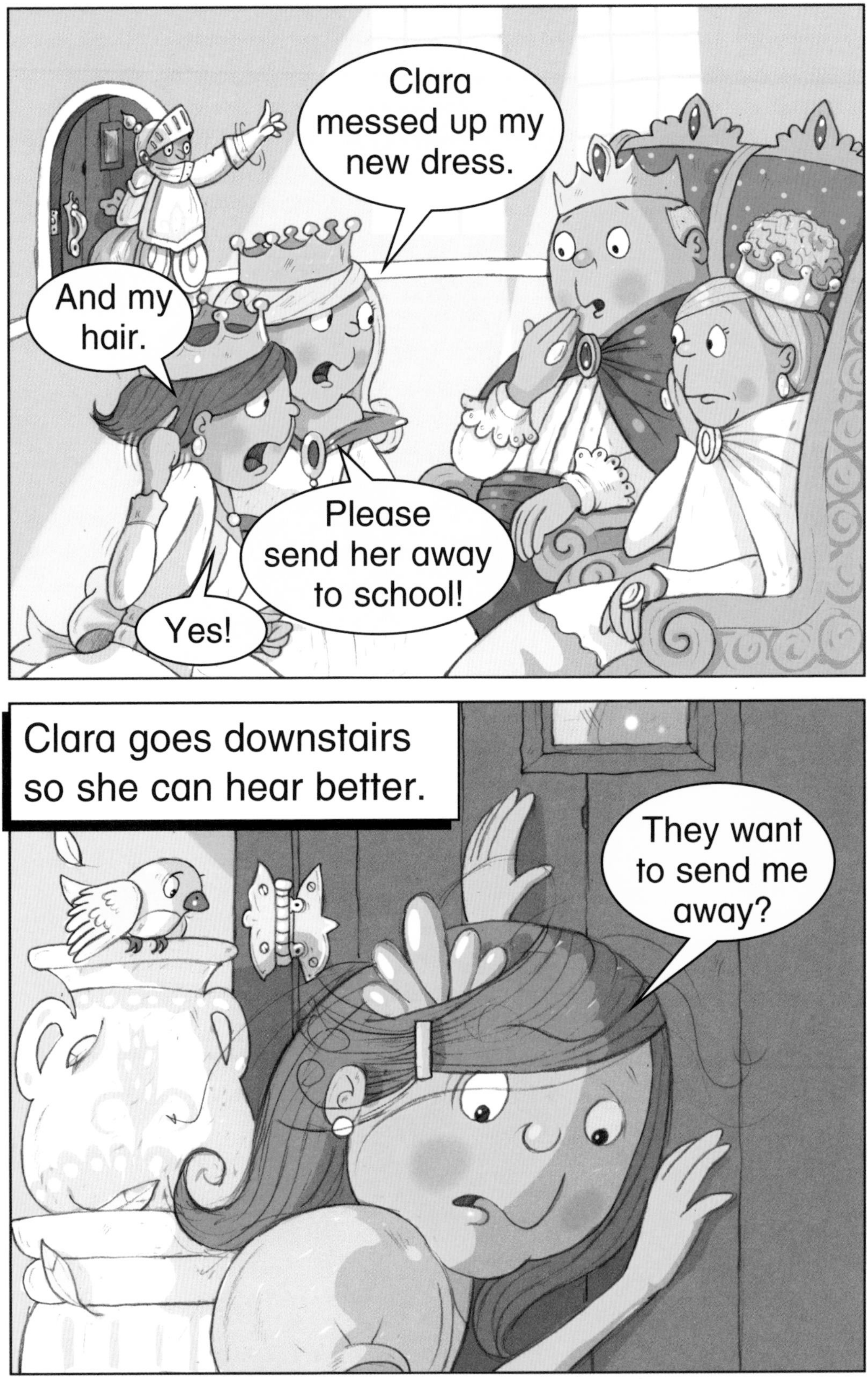
Clara messed up my new dress.
And my hair.
Please send her away to school!
Yes!
Clara goes downstairs so she can hear better.
They want to send me away?

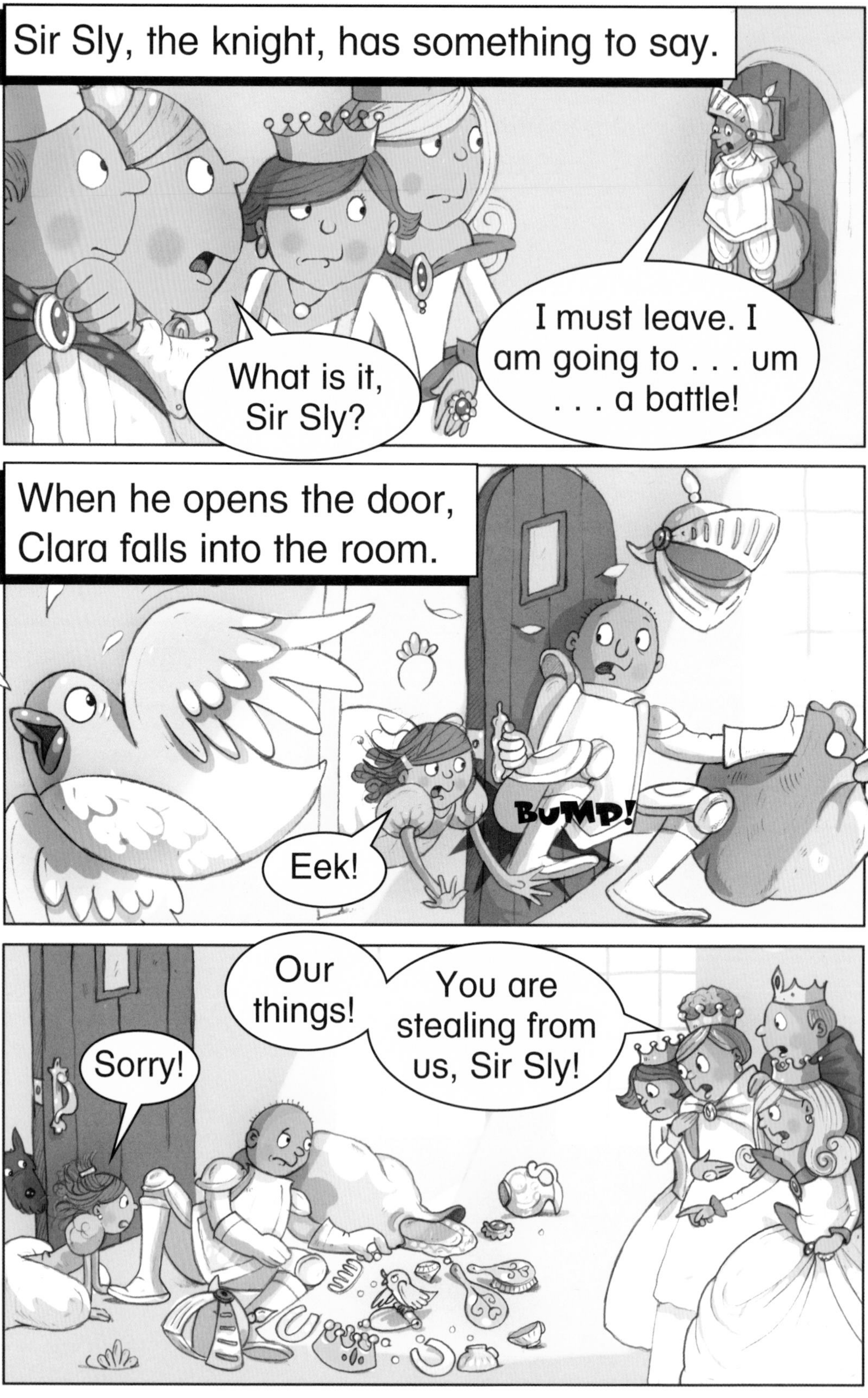
Sir Sly, the knight, has something to say.
What is it, Sir Sly?
I must leave. I am going to . . . um . . . a battle!
When he opens the door, Clara falls into the room.
Eek!
BUMP!
Our things!
You are stealing from us, Sir Sly!
Sorry!

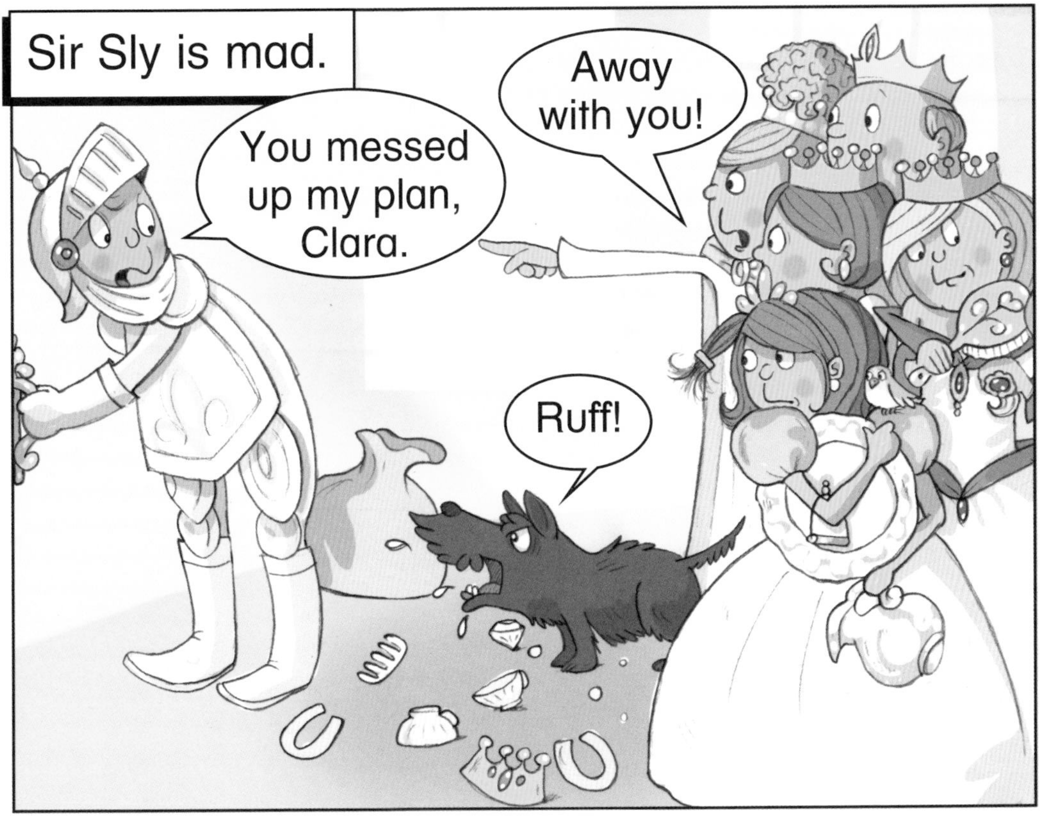
Sir Sly is mad.
You messed up my plan, Clara.
Away with you!
Ruff!

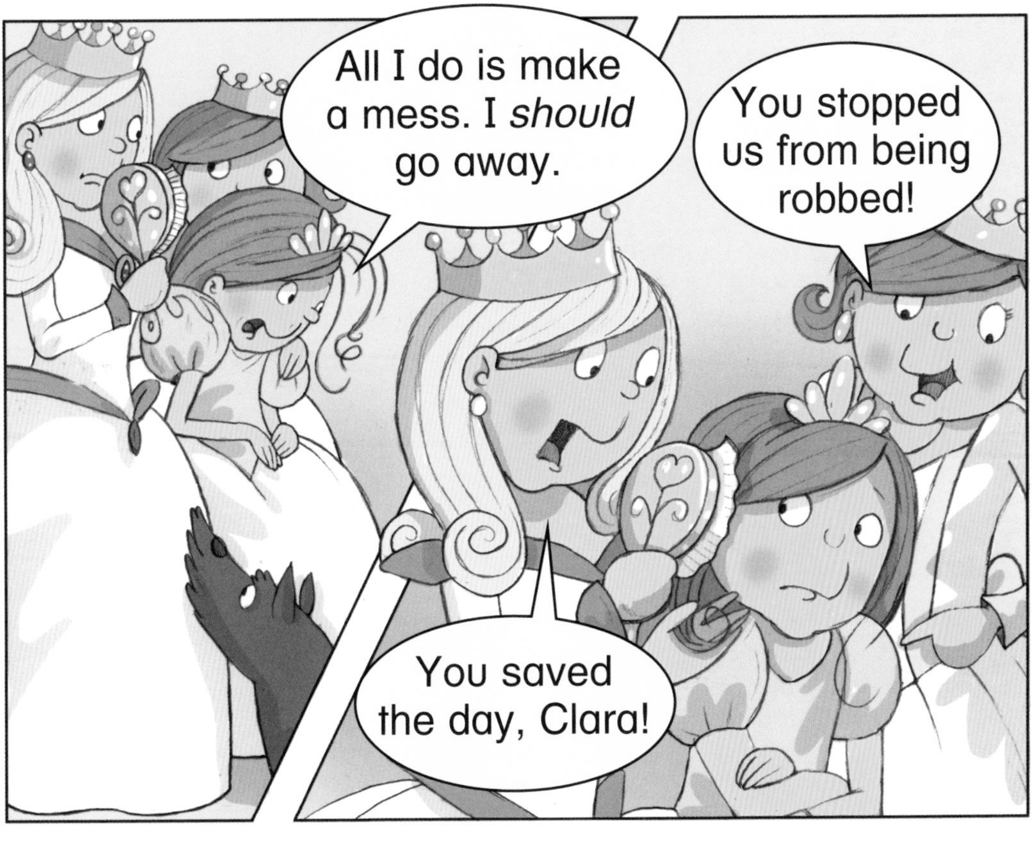
All I do is make a mess. I *should* go away.
You stopped us from being robbed!
You saved the day, Clara!

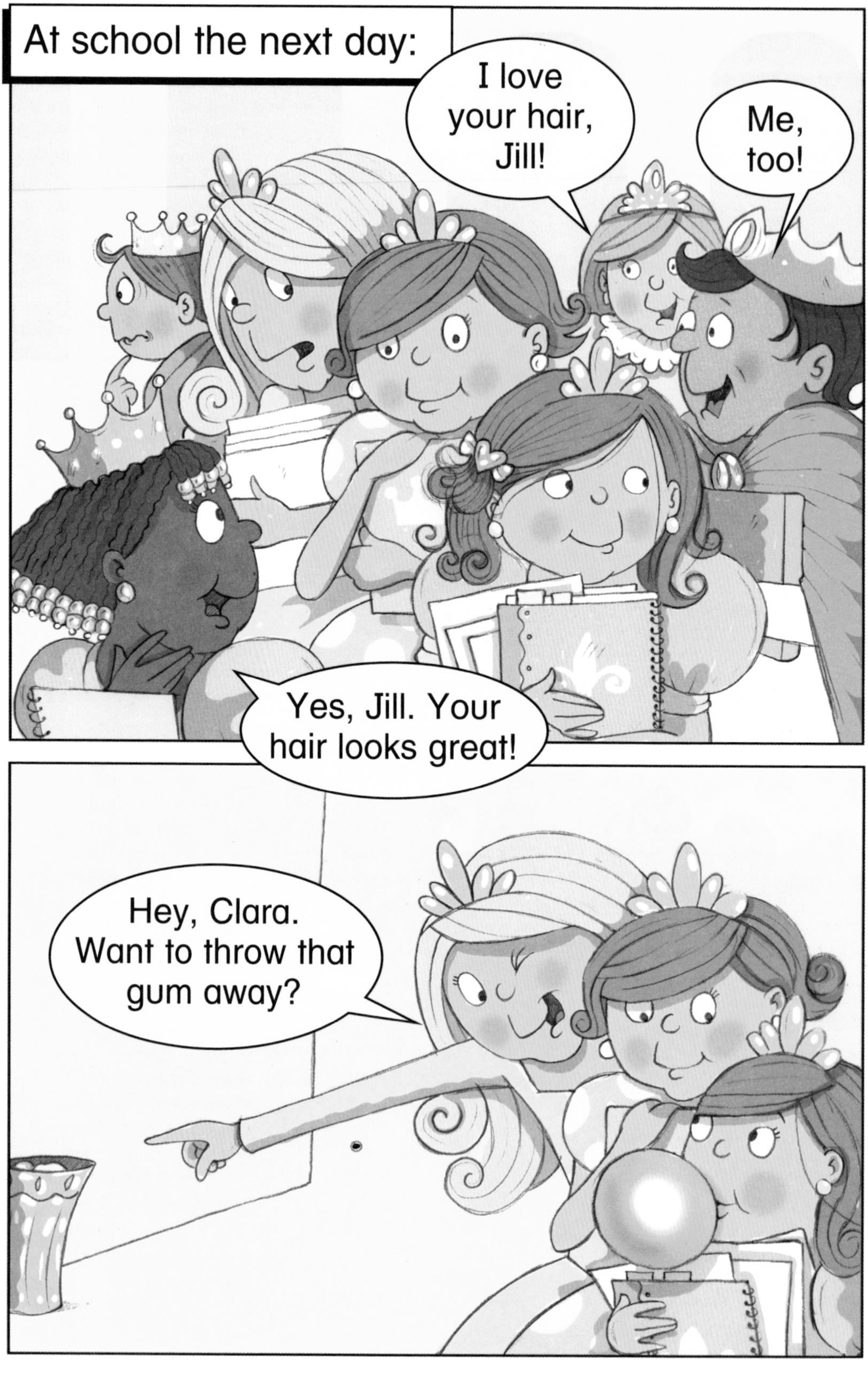
At school the next day:
I love your hair, Jill!
Me, too!
Yes, Jill. Your hair looks great!
Hey, Clara. Want to throw that gum away?

Clara's Cake

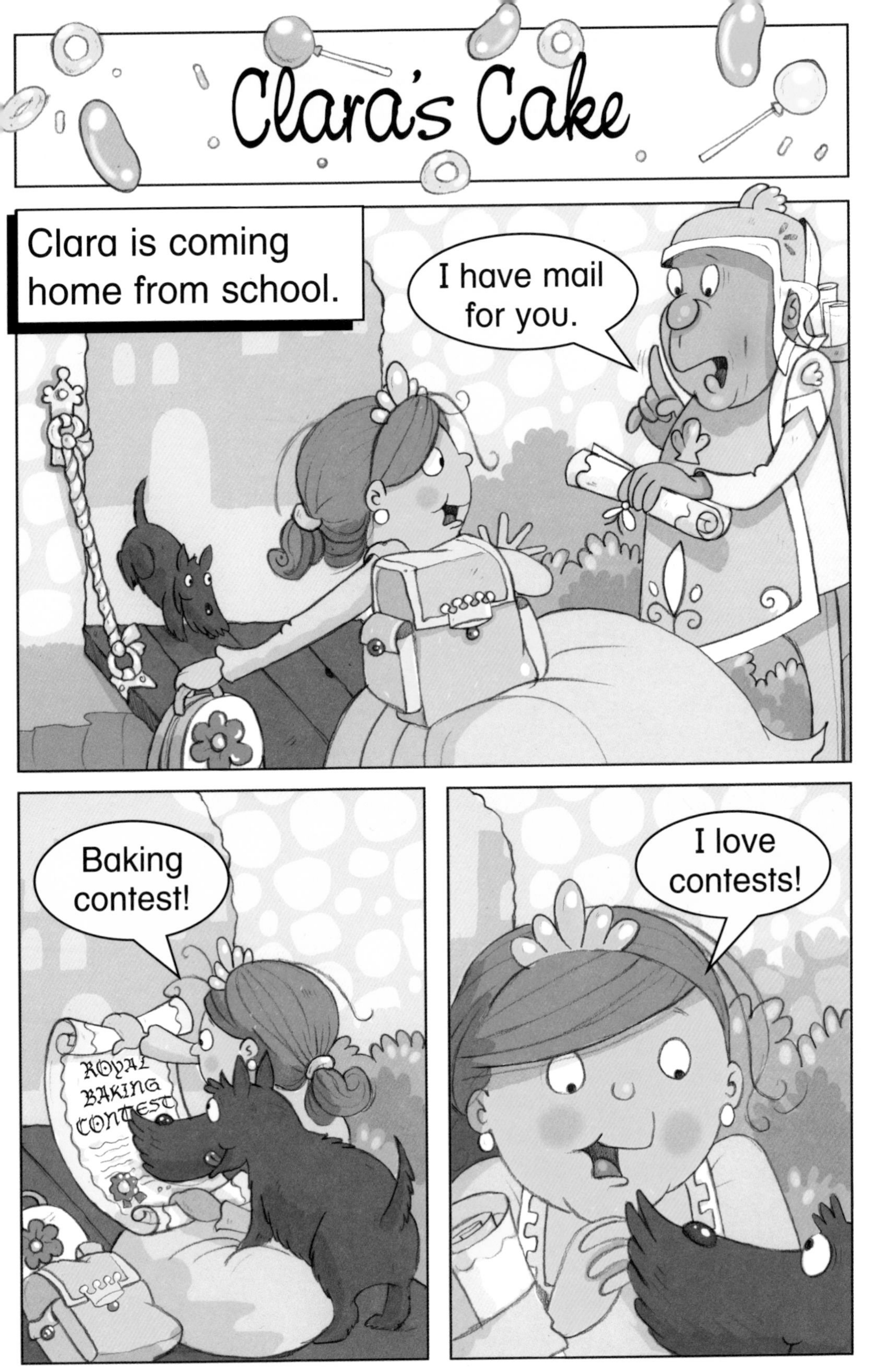
Clara is coming home from school.
I have mail for you.
Baking contest!
ROYAL BAKING CONTEST
I love contests!

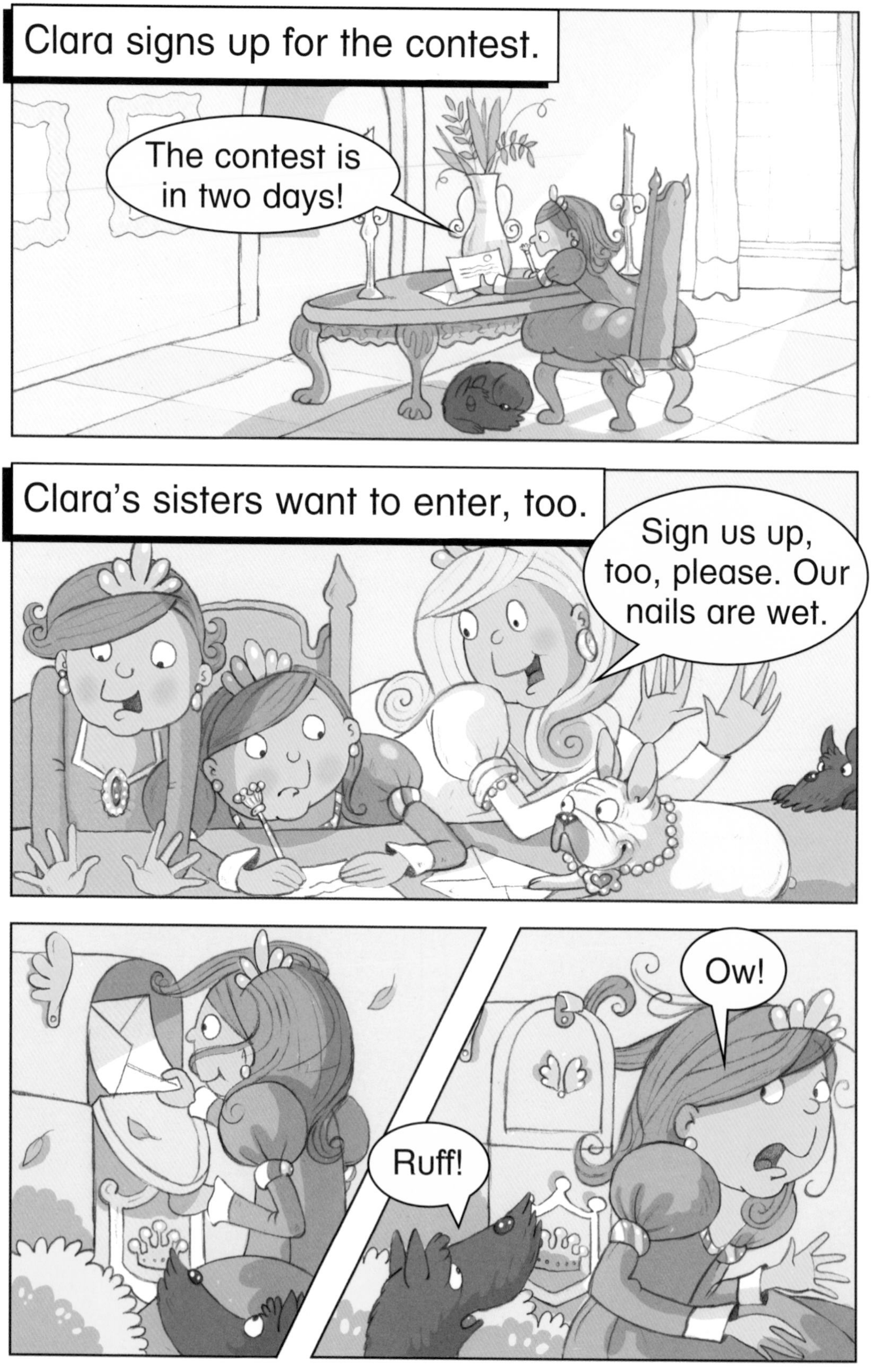
Clara signs up for the contest.
The contest is in two days!
Clara's sisters want to enter, too.
Sign us up, too, please. Our nails are wet.
Ruff!
Ow!

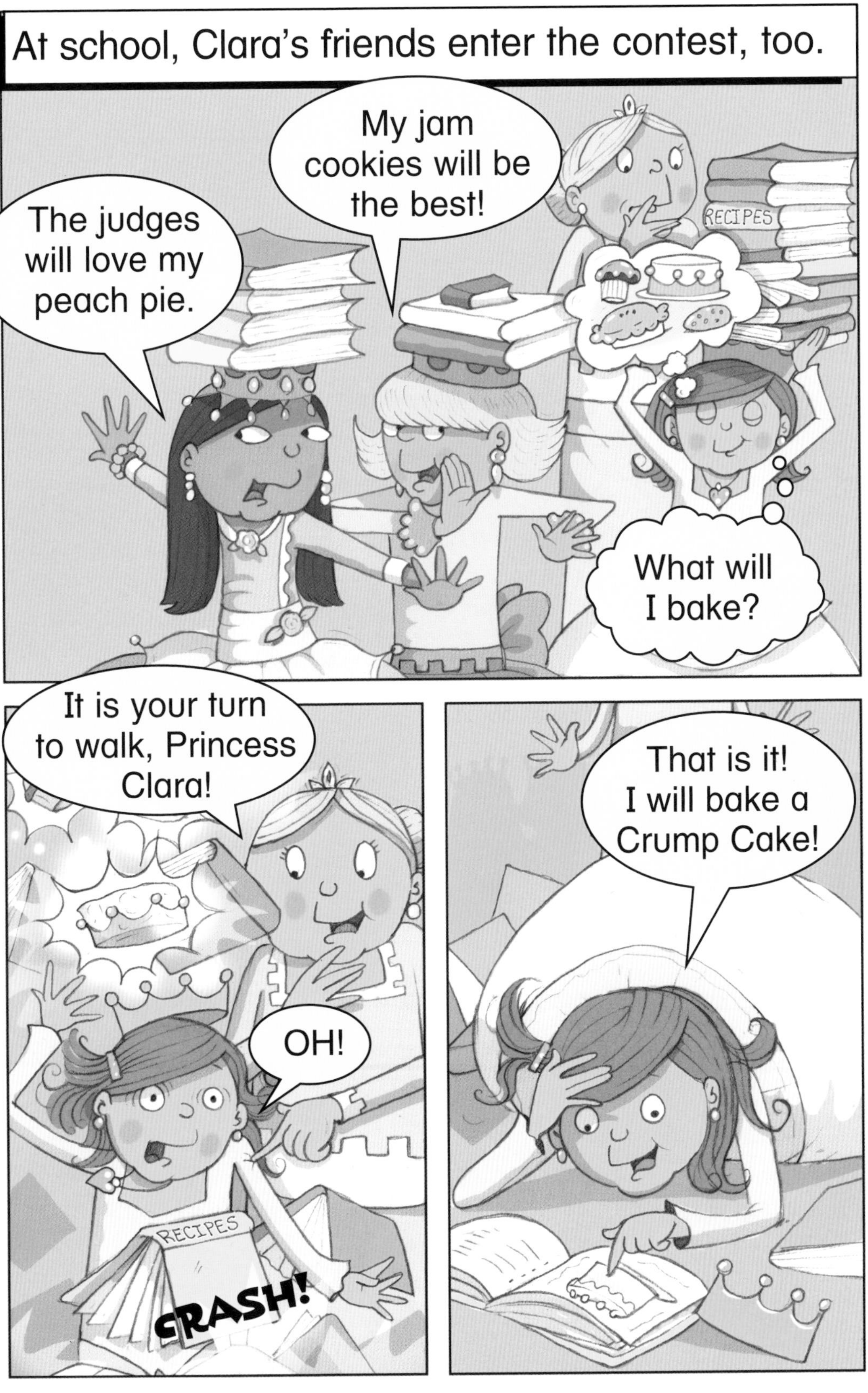
At school, Clara's friends enter the contest, too.
The judges will love my peach pie.
My jam cookies will be the best!
RECIPES
What will I bake?
It is your turn to walk, Princess Clara!
OH!
RECIPES
CRASH!
That is it! I will bake a Crump Cake!

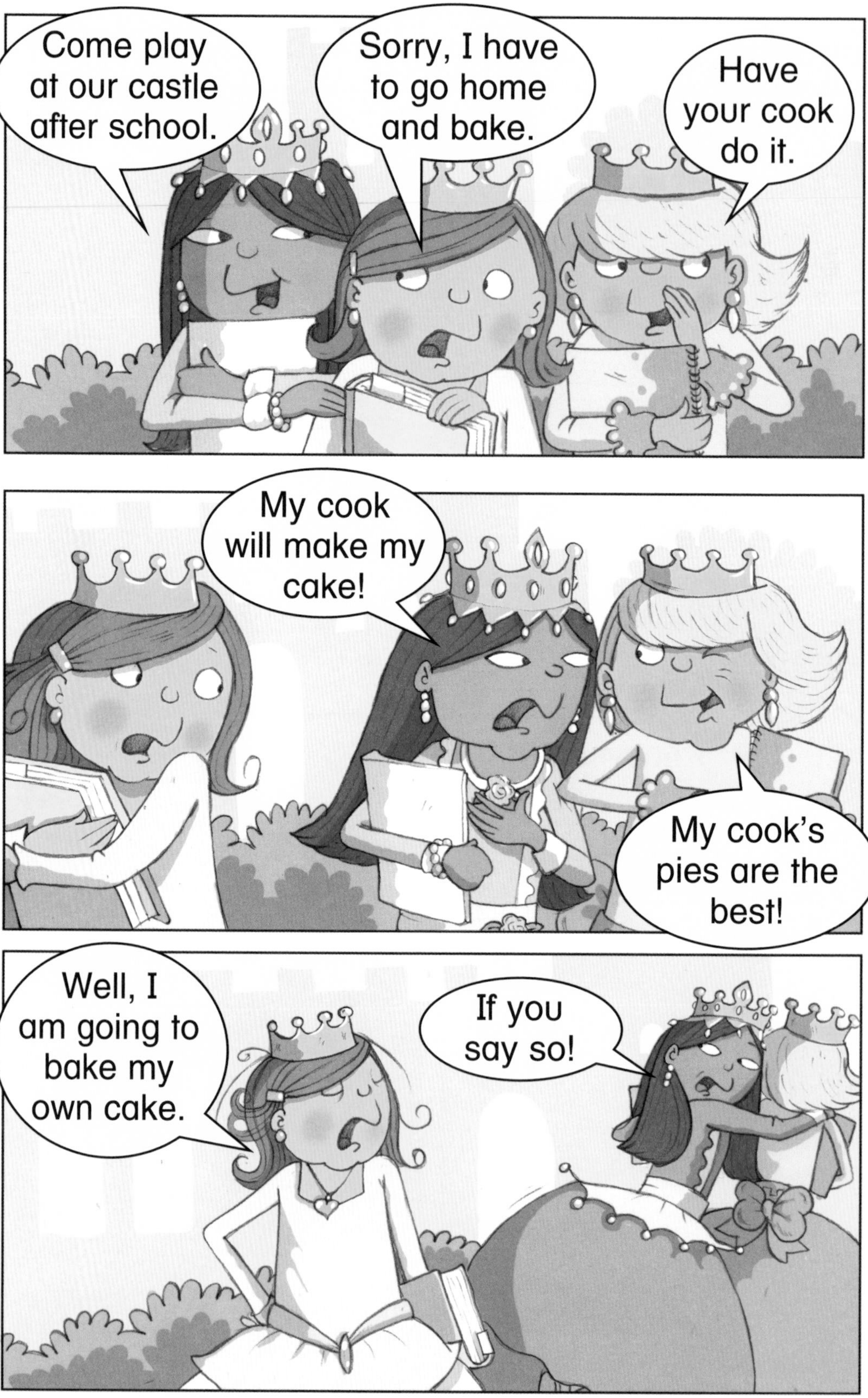
Come play at our castle after school.
Sorry, I have to go home and bake.
Have your cook do it.
My cook will make my cake!
My cook's pies are the best!
Well, I am going to bake my own cake.
If you say so!

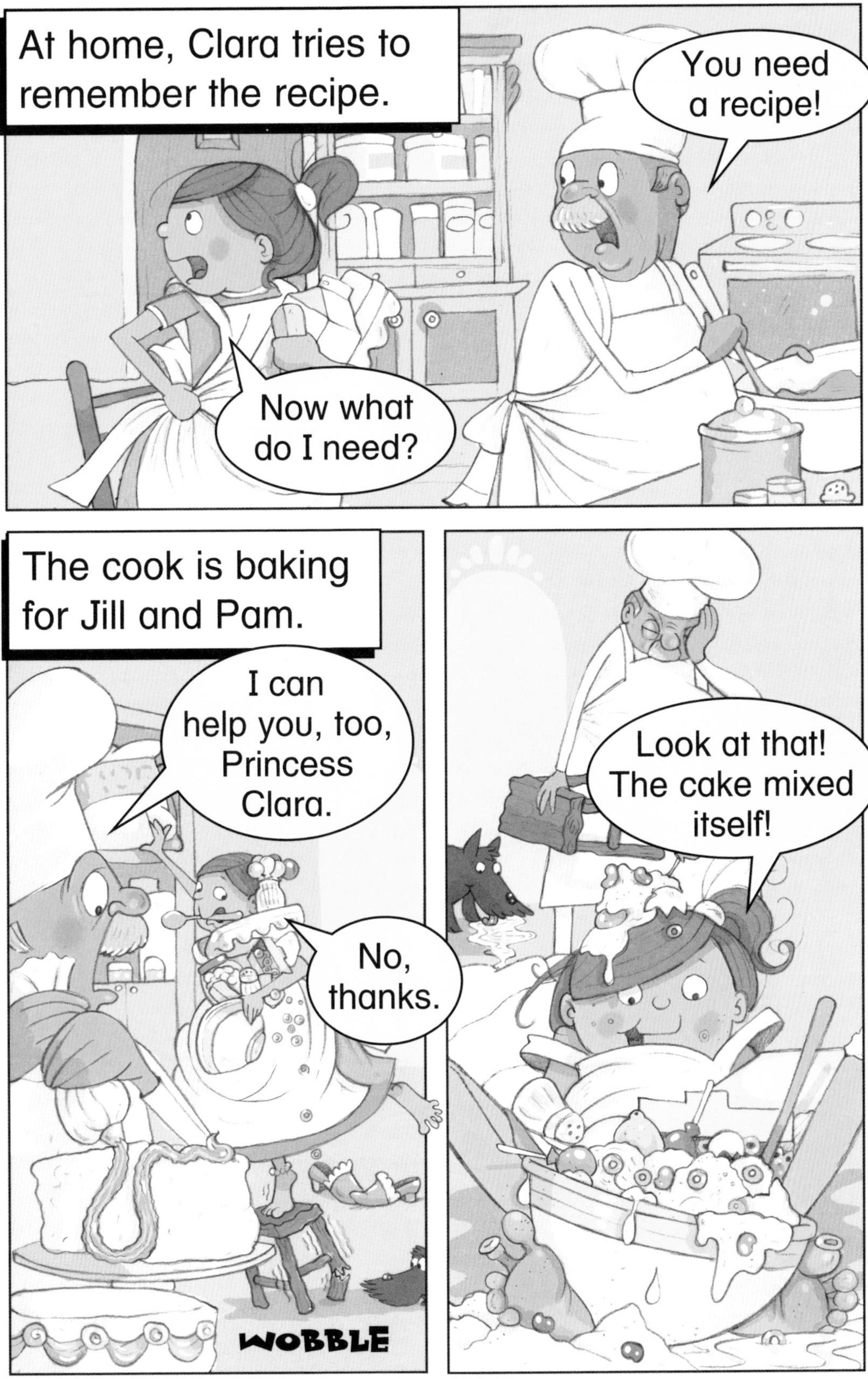
At home, Clara tries to remember the recipe.
Now what do I need?
You need a recipe!
The cook is baking for Jill and Pam.
I can help you, too, Princess Clara.
No, thanks.
WOBBLE
Look at that! The cake mixed itself!

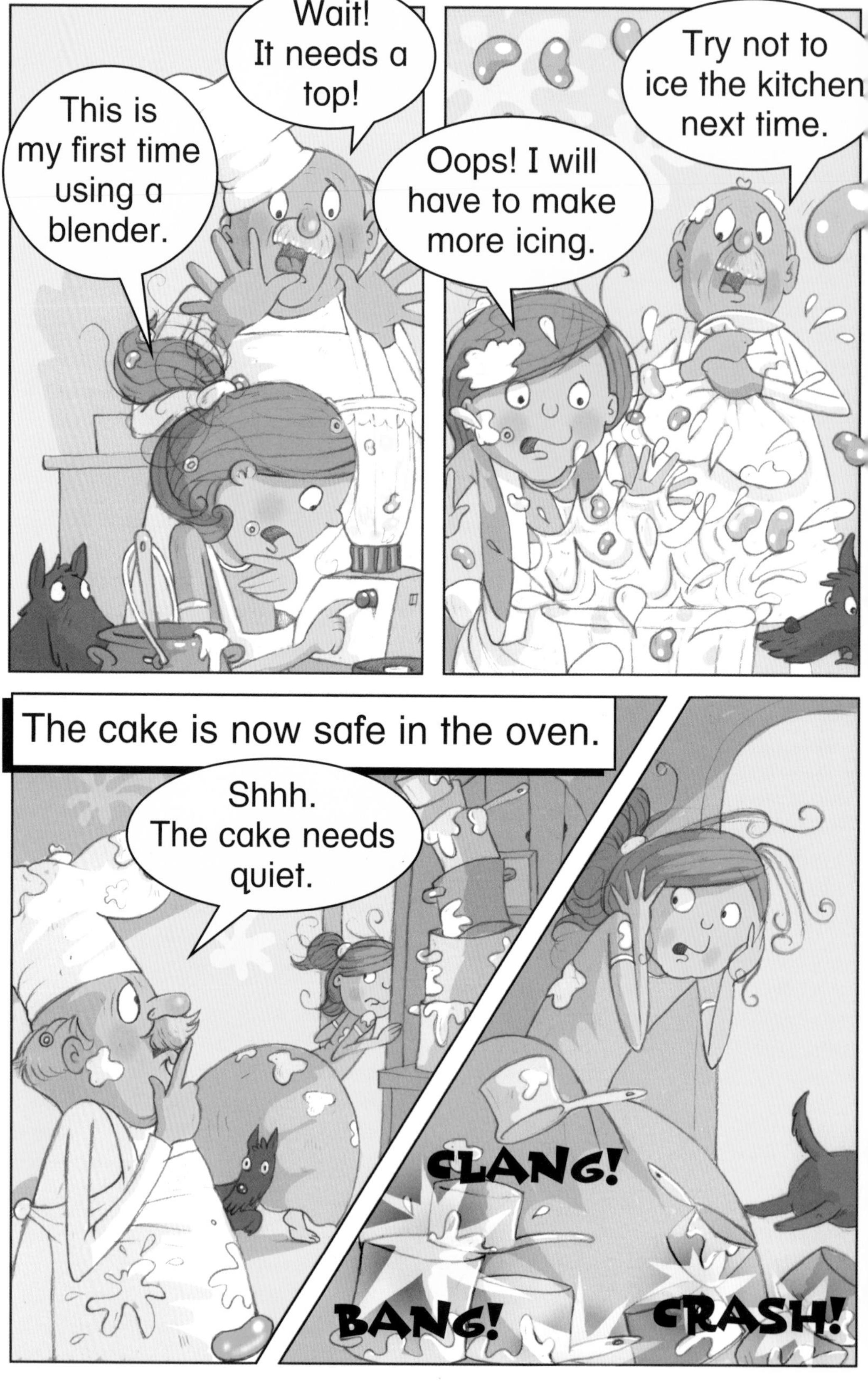
Wait! It needs a top!
This is my first time using a blender.
Try not to ice the kitchen next time.
Oops! I will have to make more icing.
The cake is now safe in the oven.
Shhh. The cake needs quiet.
CLANG!
BANG!
CRASH!

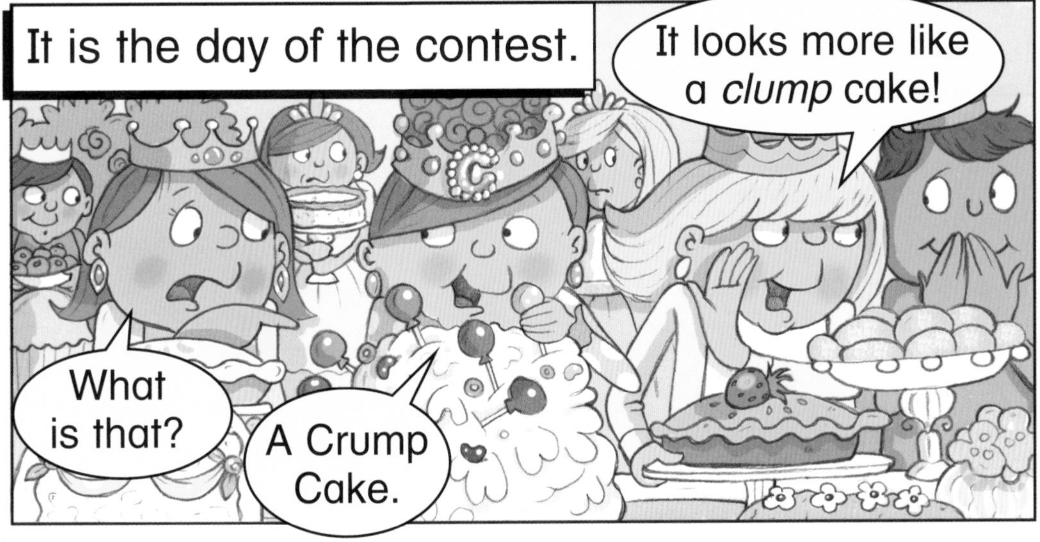
It is the day of the contest.
It looks more like a *clump* cake!
What is that?
A Crump Cake.

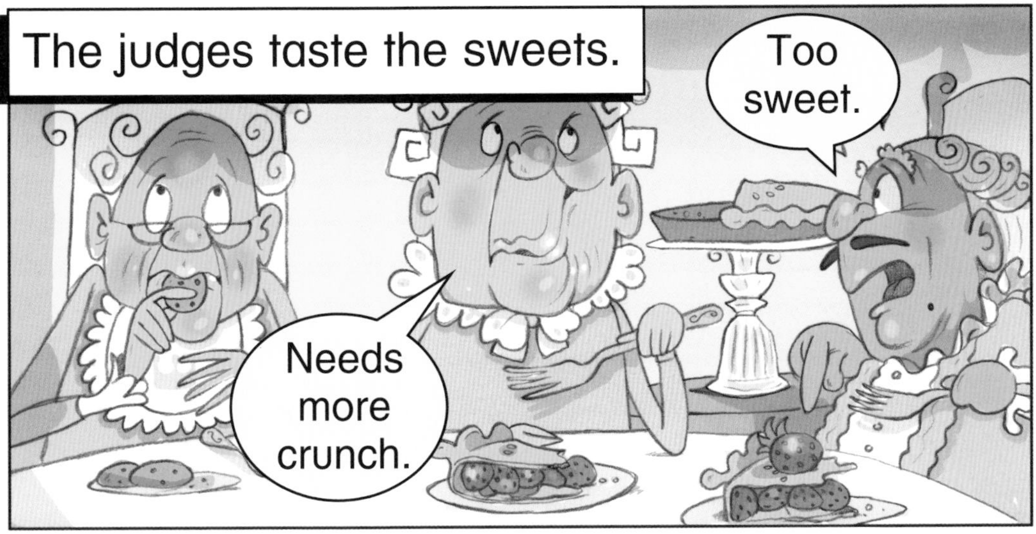
The judges taste the sweets.
Too sweet.
Needs more crunch.

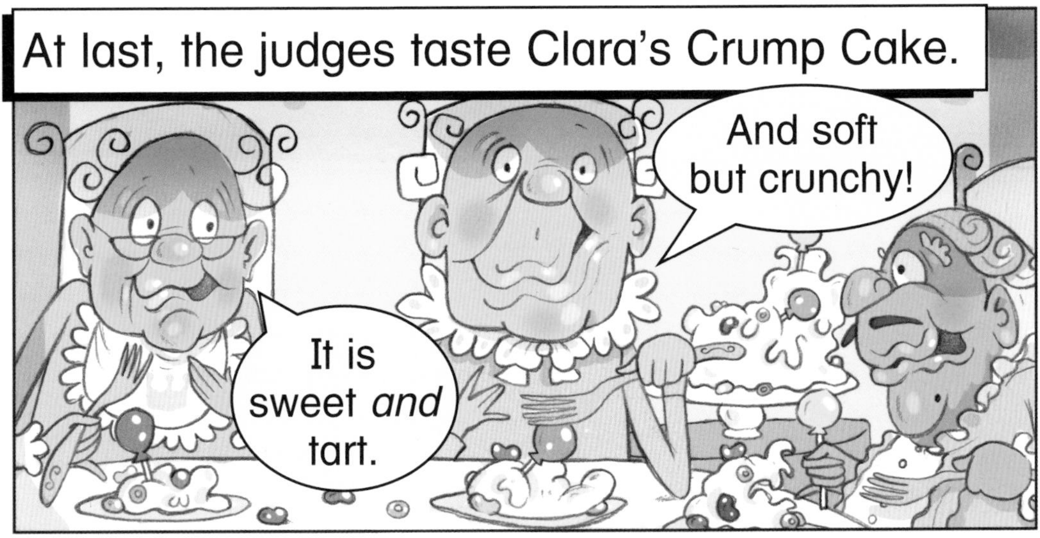
At last, the judges taste Clara's Crump Cake.
It is sweet *and* tart.
And soft but crunchy!

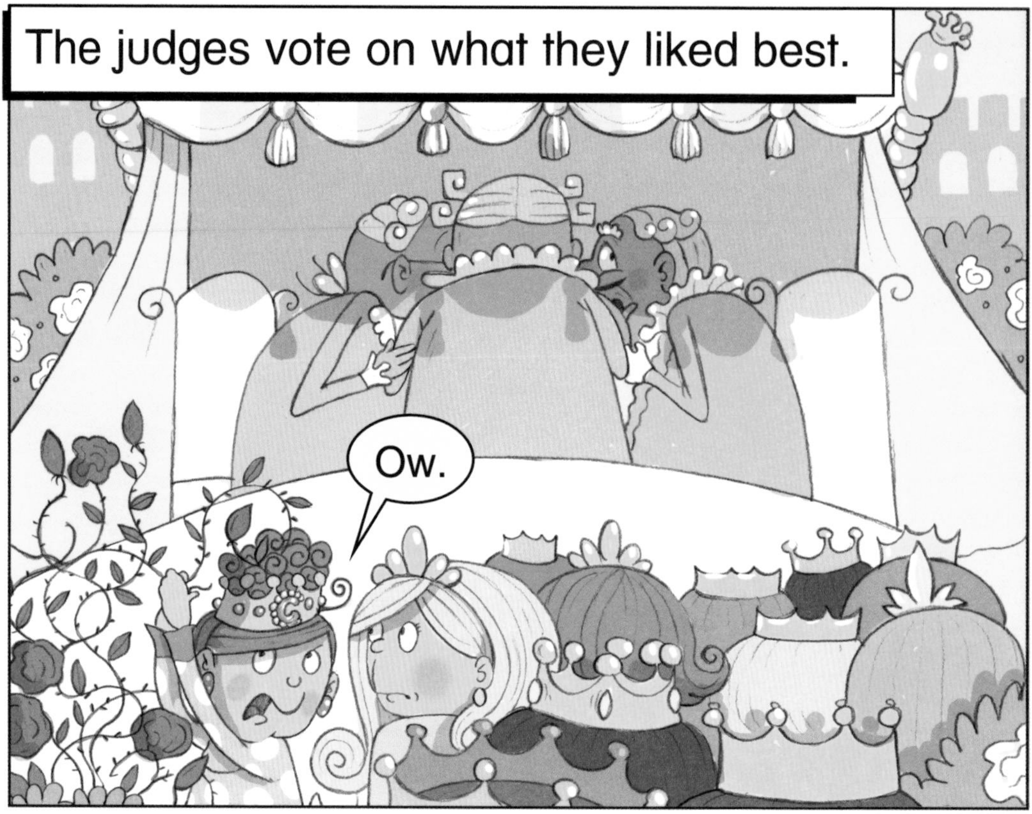

The judges vote on what they liked best.
Ow.

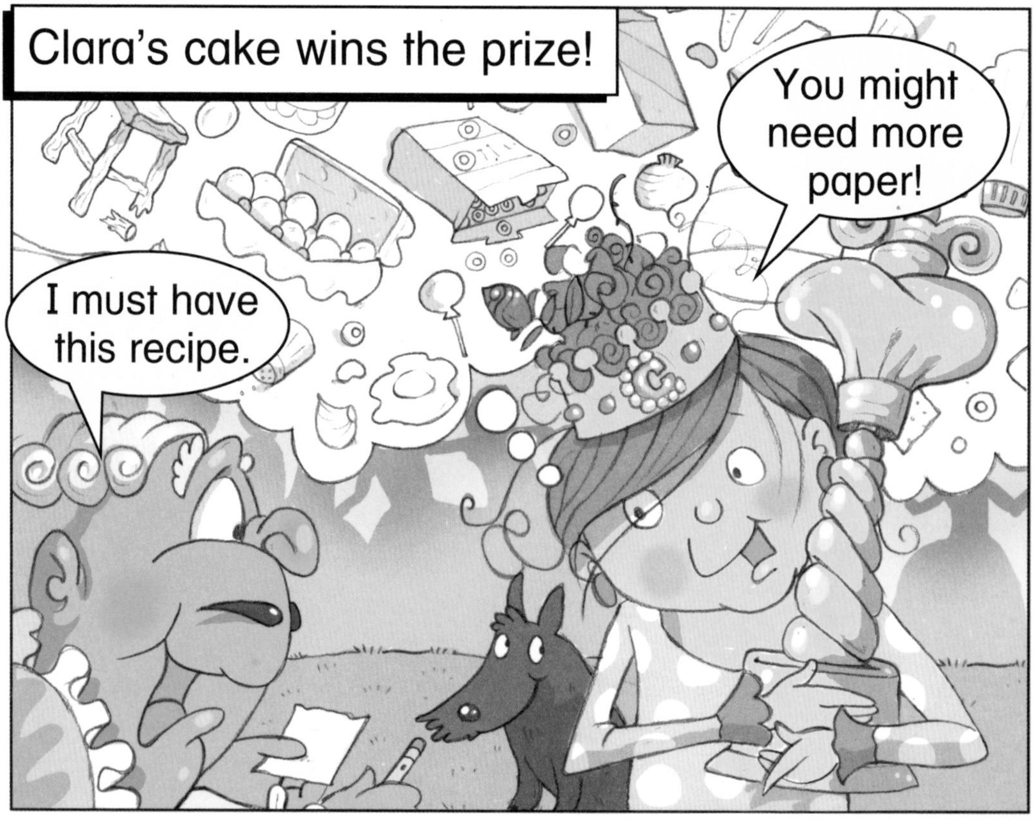

Clara's cake wins the prize!
You might need more paper!
I must have this recipe.

Clara Saves the Day

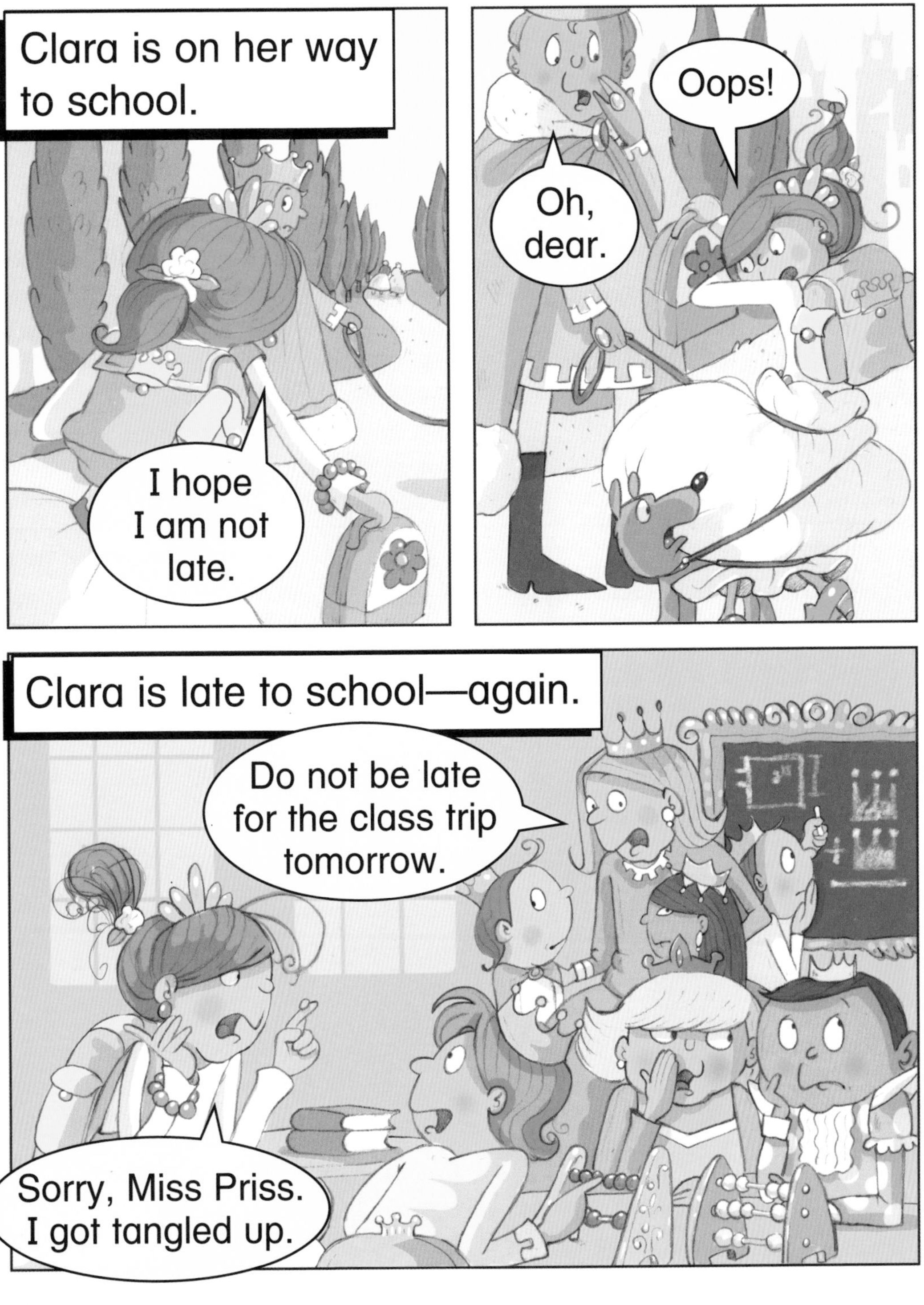
Clara is on her way to school.
I hope I am not late.
Oh, dear.
Oops!
Clara is late to school—again.
Do not be late for the class trip tomorrow.
Sorry, Miss Priss. I got tangled up.

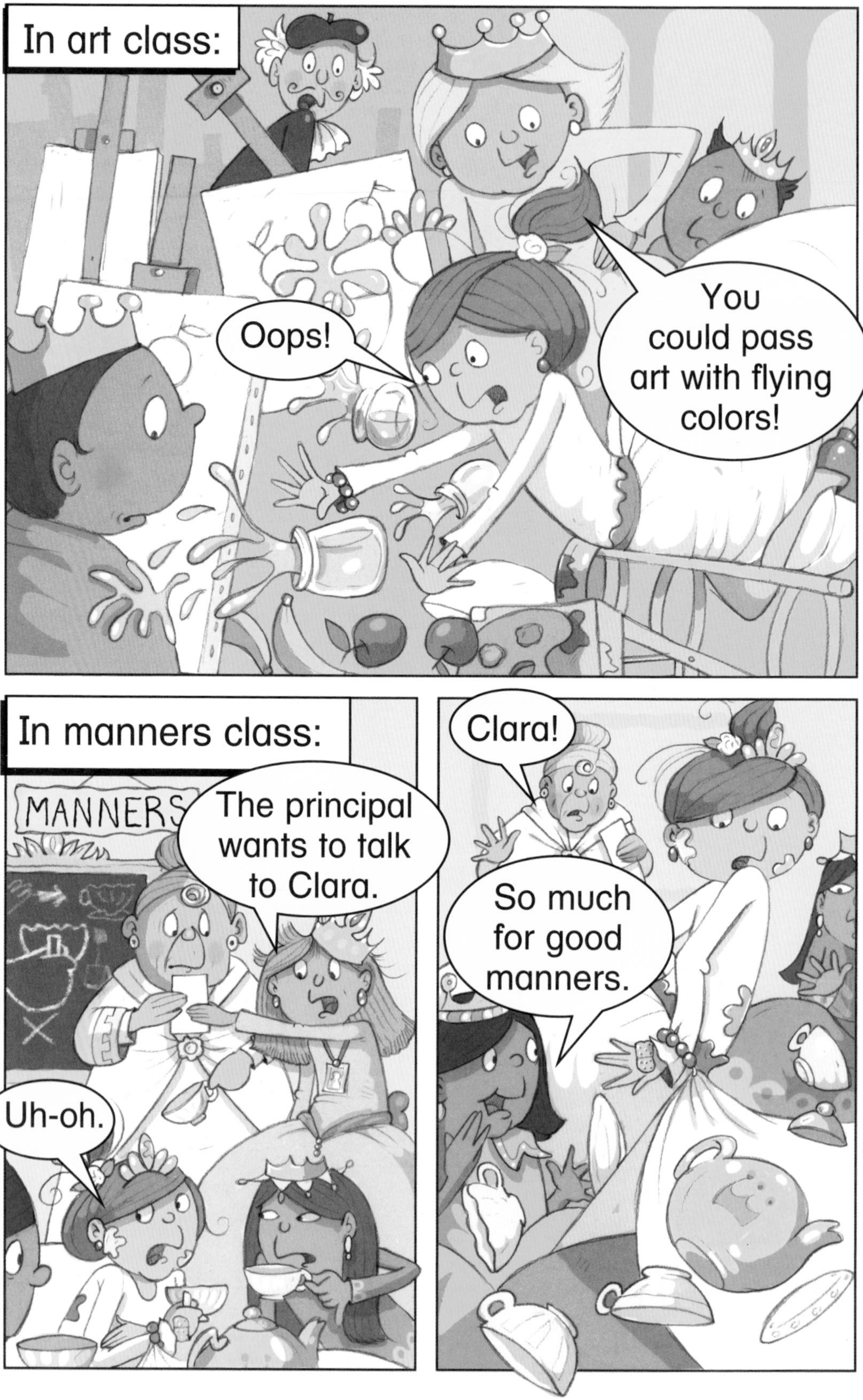
In art class:
Oops!
You could pass art with flying colors!
In manners class:
MANNERS
The principal wants to talk to Clara.
Uh-oh.
Clara!
So much for good manners.

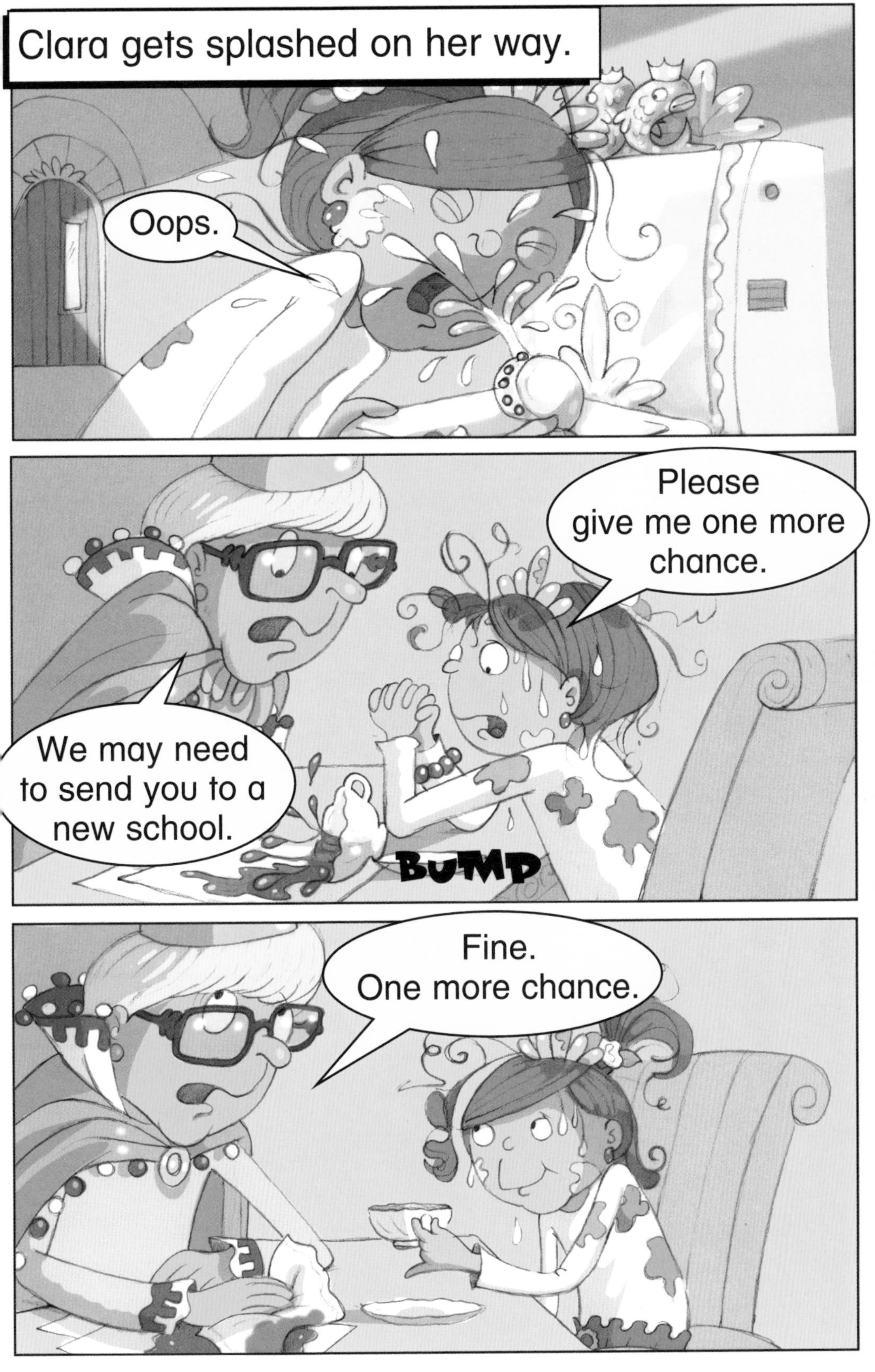
Clara gets splashed on her way.
Oops.
Please give me one more chance.
We may need to send you to a new school.
BUMP
Fine. One more chance.

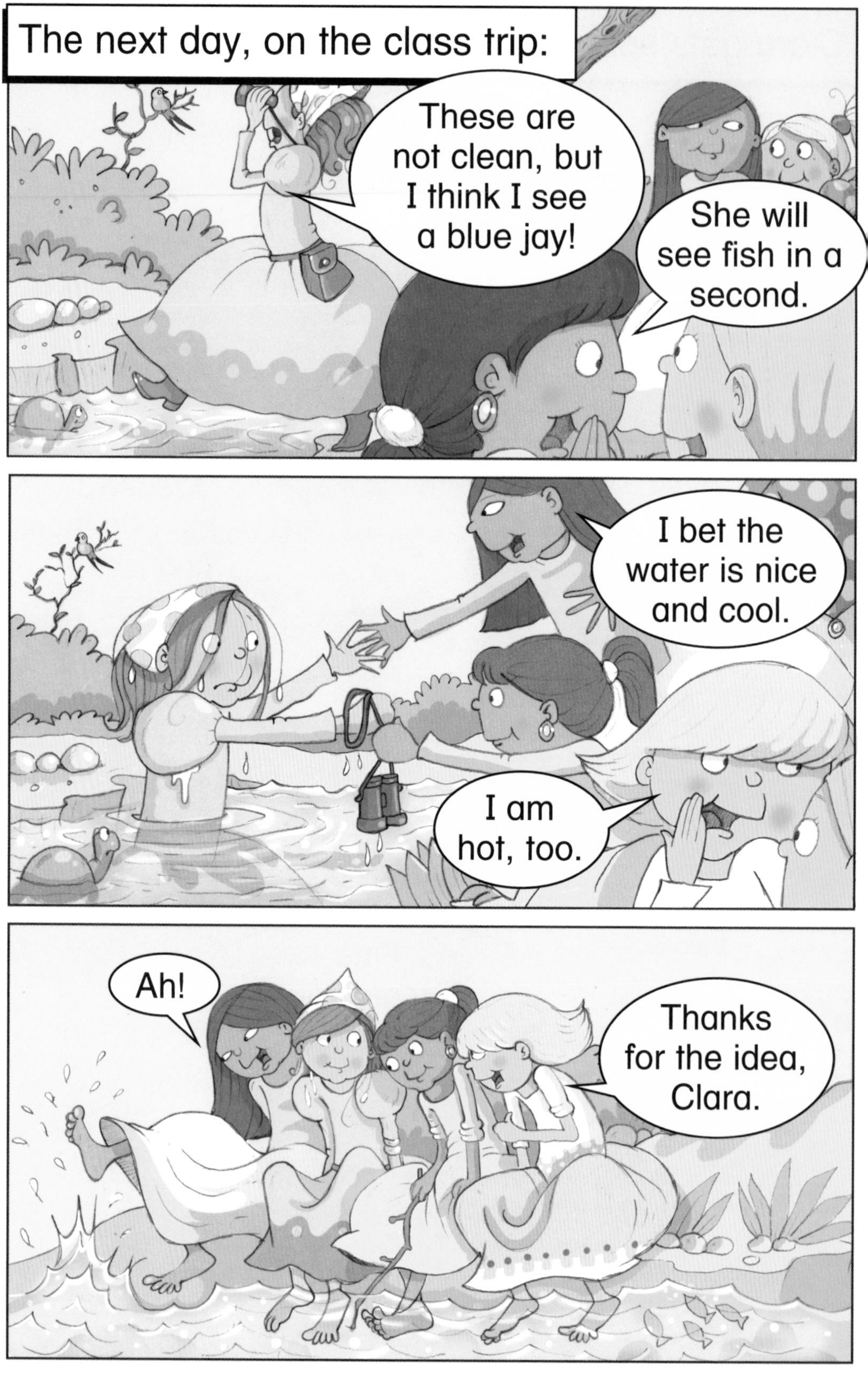
The next day, on the class trip:
These are not clean, but I think I see a blue jay!
She will see fish in a second.
I bet the water is nice and cool.
I am hot, too.
Ah!
Thanks for the idea, Clara.

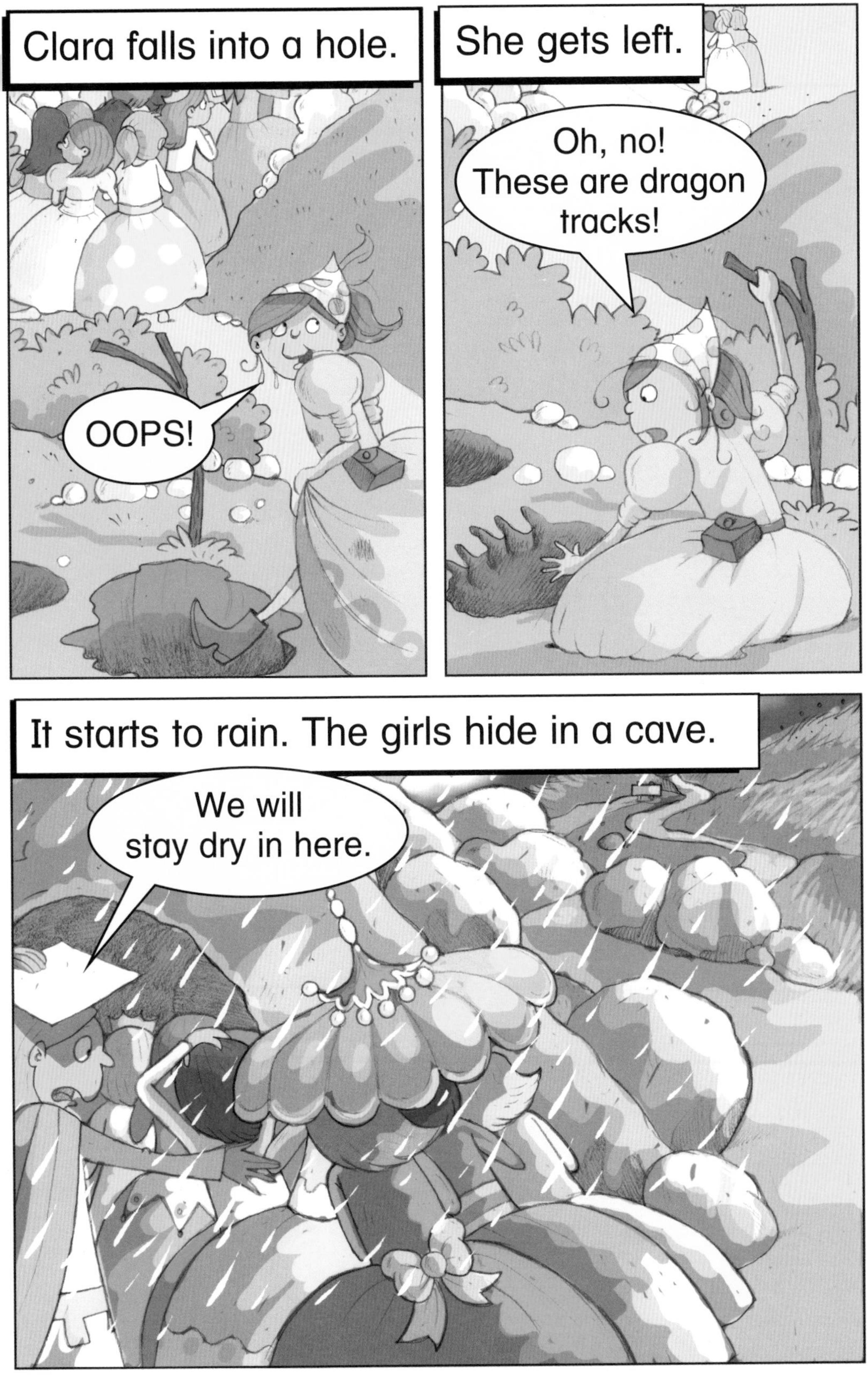
Clara falls into a hole.
OOPS!
She gets left.
Oh, no! These are dragon tracks!
It starts to rain. The girls hide in a cave.
We will stay dry in here.

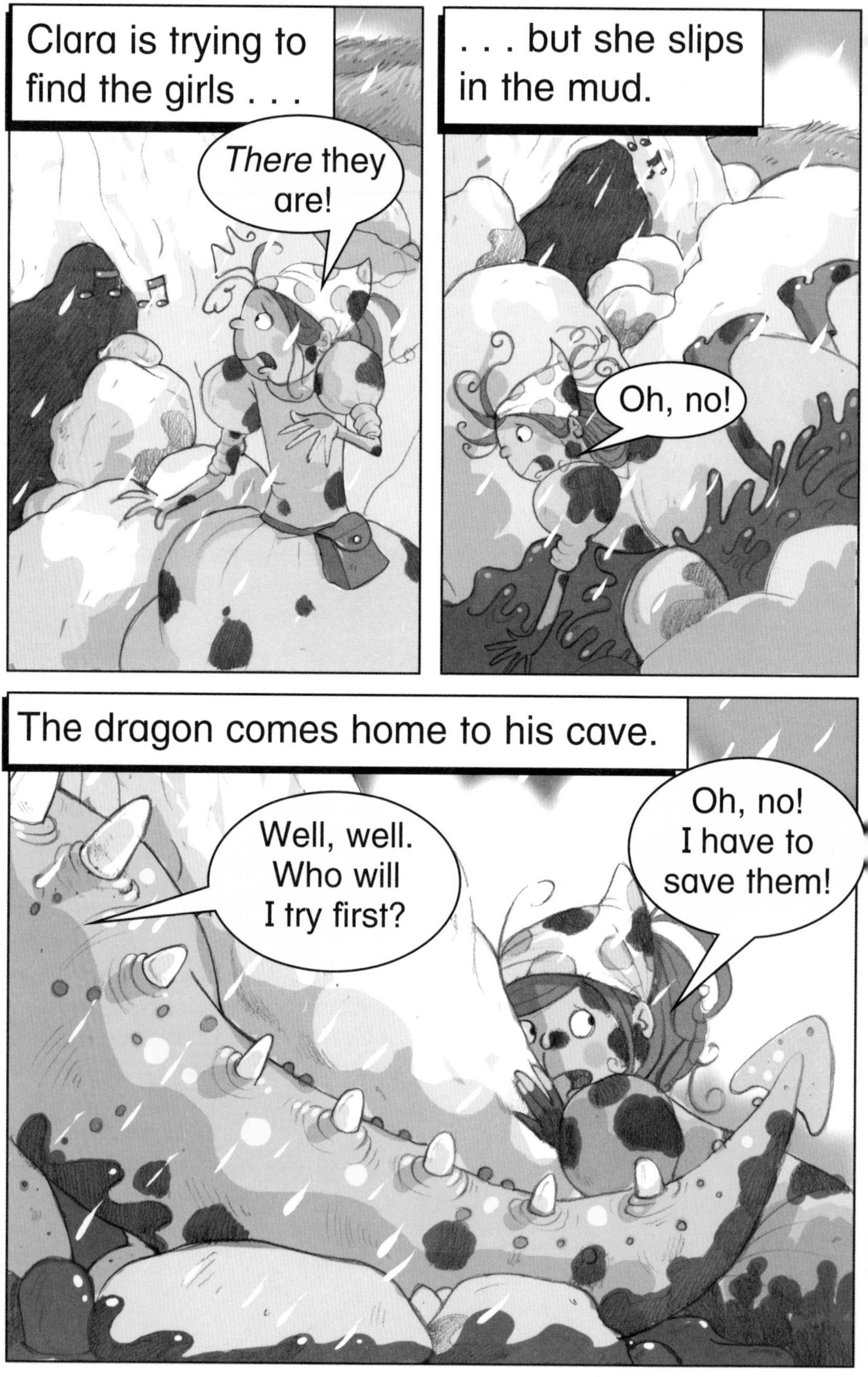
Clara is trying to find the girls . . .
There they are!
. . . but she slips in the mud.
Oh, no!
The dragon comes home to his cave.
Well, well. Who will I try first?
Oh, no! I have to save them!

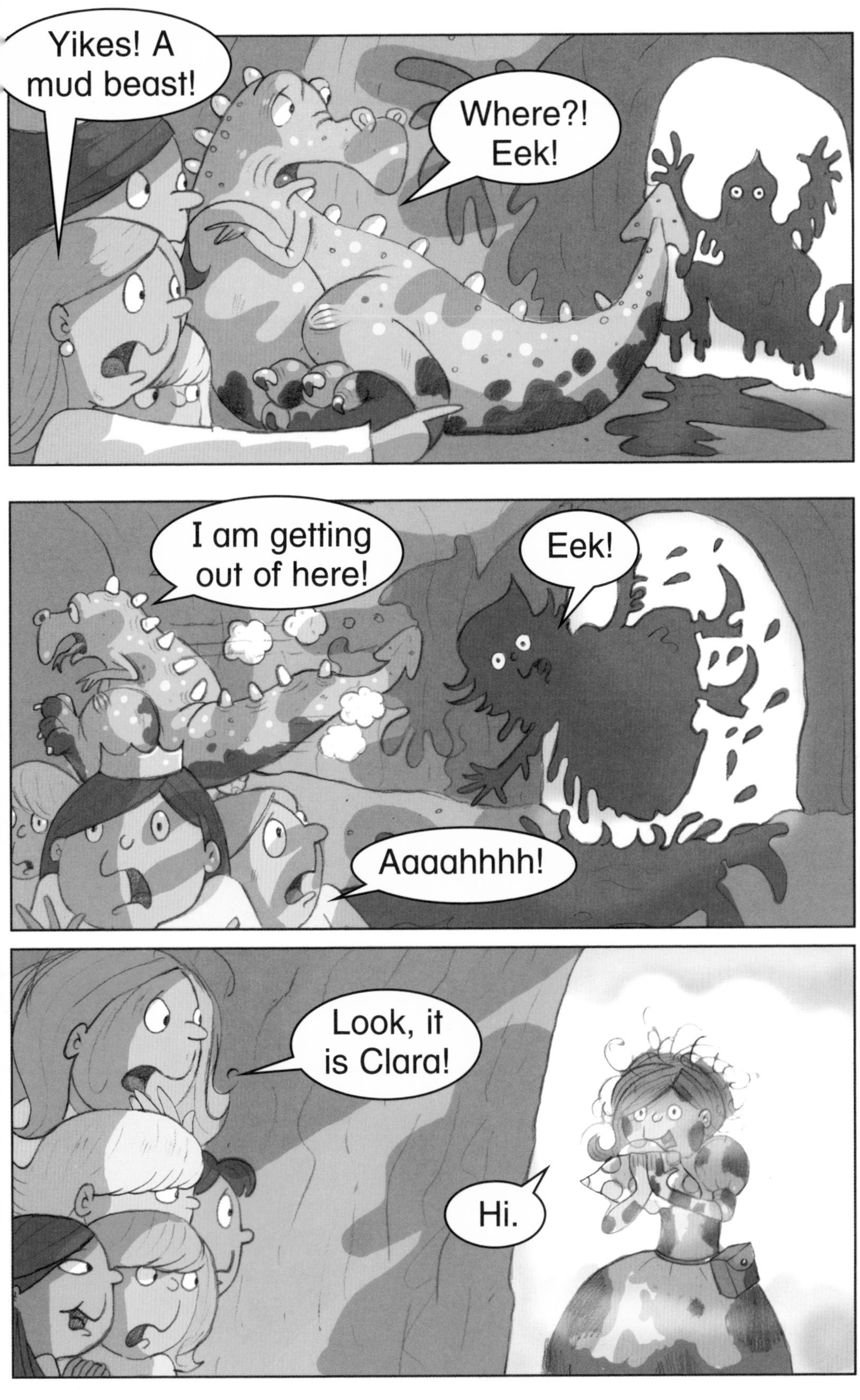
Yikes! A mud beast!
Where?! Eek!
I am getting out of here!
Eek!
Aaaahhhh!
Look, it is Clara!
Hi.

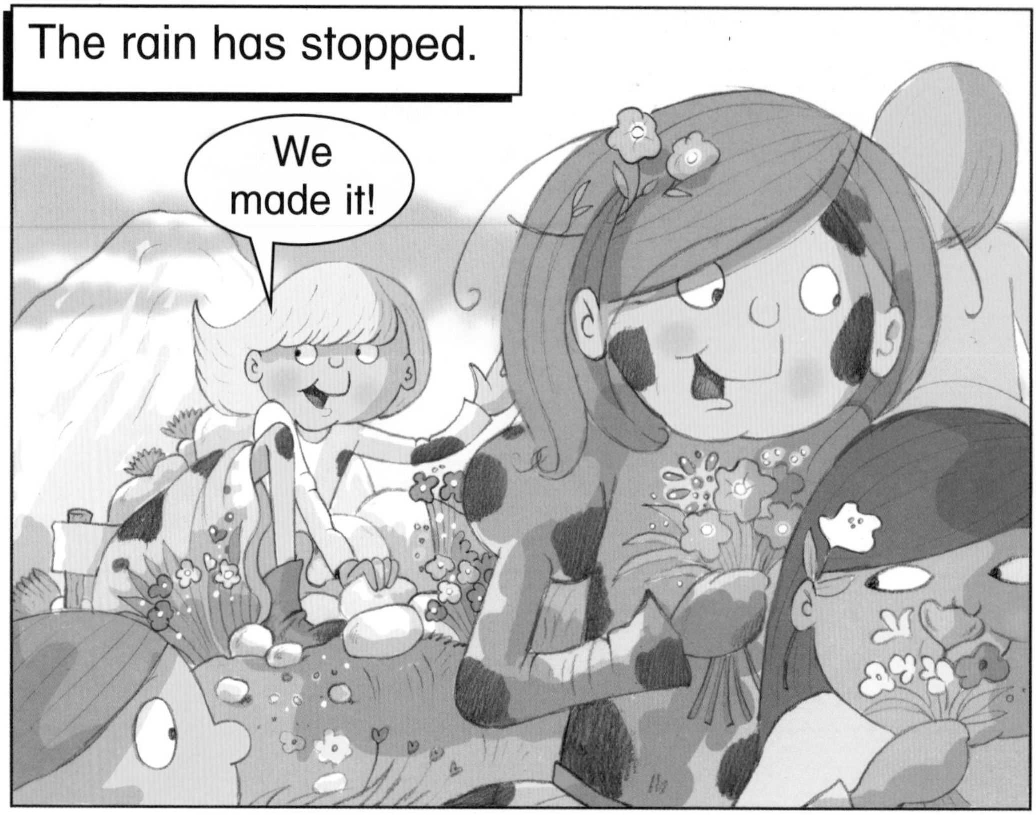
The rain has stopped.
We made it!

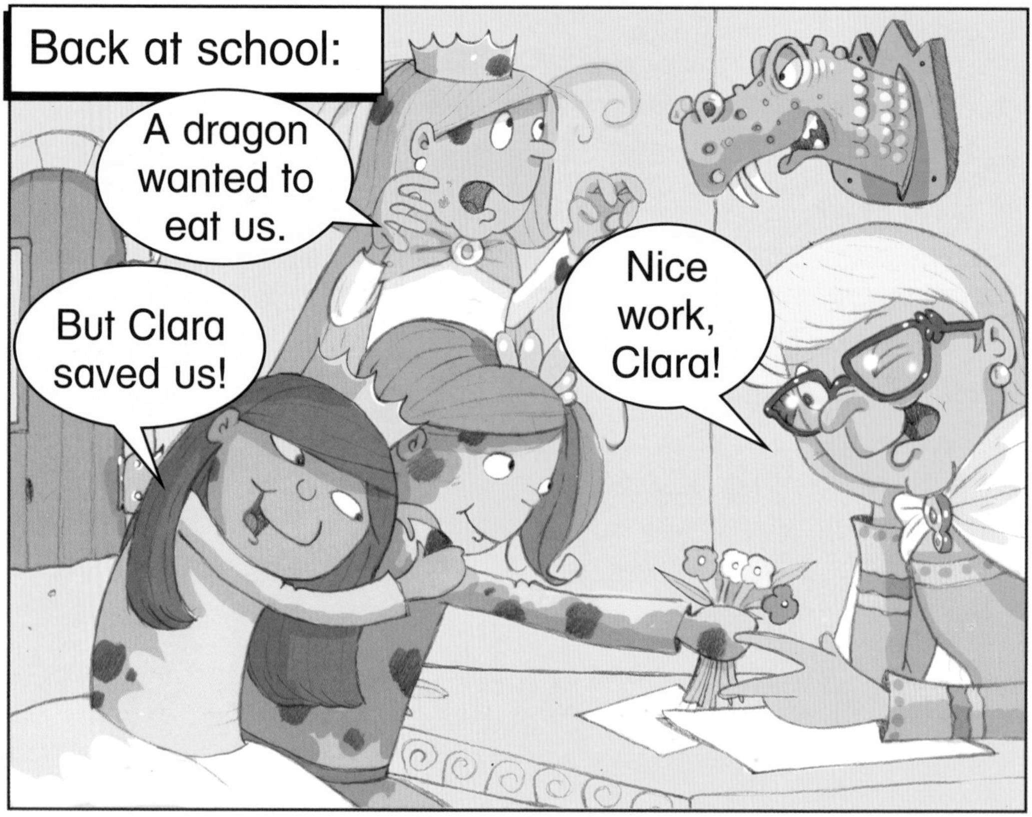
Back at school:
A dragon wanted to eat us.
But Clara saved us!
Nice work, Clara!